Why Do Dogs Drool?

And Other Questions Kids Have About Dogs

by Suzanne Slade illustrated by Cary Pillo

PICTURE WINDOW BOOKS
a capstone imprint

Special thanks to our advisers for their expertise:

Sue Lowum, DVM, Assistant Clinical Professor
University of Minnesota

Terry Flaherty, Ph.D., Professor of English
Minnesota State University, Mankato

Editor: Jill Kalz
Designer: Tracy Davies
Art Director: Nathan Gassman
Production Specialist: Jane Klenk
The illustrations in this book were created with mixed media.

Picture Window Books
151 Good Counsel Drive
P.O. Box 669
Mankato, MN 56002-0669
877-845-8392
www.picturewindowbooks.com

Printed in the United States of America in North Mankato, Minnesota.
092009
005618CGS10

All books published by Picture Window Books are manufactured with paper containing at least 10 percent post-consumer waste.

Library of Congress Cataloging-in-Publication Data
Slade, Suzanne.
Why do dogs drool? : and other questions kids have about dogs / by Suzanne Slade ; illustrated by Cary Pillo.
p. cm. — (Kids' questions)
Includes index.
ISBN 978-1-4048-5762-9 (library binding)
ISBN 978-1-4048-6103-9 (paperback)
1. Dogs—Miscellanea—Juvenile literature. I. Pillo, Cary, ill. II. Title.
SF426.5.S576 2010
636.7—dc22 2009031833

How many different types of dogs are there?

Audrey, age 9

There are more than 450 different types, or breeds, of dogs in the world. Some breeds make good workers, but most dogs live with people as pets. In fact, dogs are the most popular pets in the United States. More than 43 million families have at least one dog in their home.

What is the biggest dog?

Keegan, age 8

How small is the smallest dog?

Rachel, age 6

The Irish Wolfhound is the tallest dog in the world. It is about 32 inches (81 centimeters) tall and weighs 120 pounds (54 kilograms). Standing 6 to 9 inches (15 to 23 cm) tall and weighing just 6 pounds (2.7 kg) or less, the Chihuahua is the smallest dog.

What is the heaviest dog in the United States?

Ashlee, age 8

The Mastiff is the heaviest dog in the United States. Most Mastiffs weigh 165 to 220 pounds (74 to 99 kg). But some can weigh more than 300 pounds (135 kg)!

Why do dogs have hair?

William, age 7

What dog has the most hair?

Angel, age 8

Hair keeps a dog warm in cold weather. It also protects a dog's skin from sharp objects. The Old English Sheepdog is one of the hairiest dogs. The Puli also has a long, shaggy coat. This dog's hair clumps together to form cords that look like pieces of rope.

Are there any dogs without hair?

Henry, age 9

Yes. One of the most popular hairless dogs is the Chinese Crested. It has soft, silky hair on its head, tail, and feet, but its body is hairless. Another hairless breed is the Xoloitzcuintli (show-low-eats-queen-tlee).

What do dogs eat?

Moises, age 6

Dogs will eat almost anything. However, most veterinarians suggest owners simply feed their dog one thing—dog food. Dog food has everything a dog needs to stay healthy. People food, such as table scraps and leftovers, can make a dog sick.

Why does my dog fart?

Izzy, age 8

Dogs sometimes produce gas as their bodies digest, or break down, food. Dogs release this gas as smelly farts!

How many teeth do dogs have?

Spencer, age 6

Most breeds have 42 teeth—20 on the top and 22 on the bottom.

How come dogs use their tongues for drinking?

2nd graders

Why do dogs drink water from the toilet?

Josie, age 8

A dog cannot hold a cup! But its long tongue works great as a scoop. A dog's tongue curls around the water and tosses it into the dog's mouth. A thirsty dog is not thinking about germs. It's just looking for the nearest water. A toilet is the right height for larger dogs to take a quick drink.

Why do they sniff a lot?

Kayla, age 8

How do dogs find the bones they hide?

Jordan, age 6

Dogs find out about the world around them by sniffing. They smell trees and fire hydrants to find out which dogs have stopped there. After giving *you* a good sniff, your dog knows where you have been, which friends you were with, and even what you ate. A dog's sense of smell is up to 100 times stronger than a person's. With a nose like that, finding bones is easy!

Why do dogs drool?

Zoe, age 7

Certain breeds drool more than others. Bassett Hounds, Saint Bernards, and Newfoundlands drool a lot. Big droolers often have loose skin around their mouths that allows saliva to drip out. Many dogs also drool when they see food.

Are they colorblind?

Joshua, age 8

No. Dogs can see colors, but not as brightly as people see them.

Why do dogs circle before they sleep?

Alicia, age 8

Do dogs have dreams?

Blake, age 8

No one knows for sure why dogs circle before going to sleep. It may come from their early days as wild animals. Circling helped a dog knock down tall grass or press snow into a cozy bed. Circling also scared away hidden enemies, such as snakes. And, yes, dogs dream. Dreaming dogs may howl, whine, or move their feet in their sleep.

What are some things dogs are afraid of?

Ryleigh, age 8

Many dogs are scared of thunder, fireworks, and other things that make loud noises. Some dogs are afraid of larger dogs or animals, and even children!

Why do they bite?

Aryanna, age 5

Some dogs bite when they feel scared or sense danger. Stay away from a growling dog or one that looks scared or angry. Also, be sure to ask a dog's owner before you try to pet it.

Why do dogs wag their tails?

Zoe, age 7

A wagging tail lets people know how a dog feels. A stiff wagging tail that goes straight up may mean a dog is angry or about to attack. If a dog is afraid, it might wag its tail between its legs. A tail that wags fast and is partway up usually means a happy dog.

Why do dogs bark?

Adam, age 8

Dogs bark to tell people and other dogs and animals a message. Some dogs bark when they want to play. Others bark if they want attention. A bark can warn that a stranger is near. If a dog senses danger, it may use its loudest bark to frighten an enemy away.

Why do dogs lick people?

Kianna, age 6

Dogs say hello by licking. A big sloppy lick lets people know a dog is friendly.

Why are dogs energetic?

Madison, age 7

Most dogs get plenty of food and rest, which gives their bodies lots of energy. It's important for dog owners to take their pets on walks and to play games such as fetch. This helps dogs burn off extra energy. Healthy dogs like to run, walk, and play. The amount of exercise a dog needs depends on its age and breed.

How do dogs swim?

ReAnna, age 5

Dogs swim by moving their paws in a forward, circular motion, called the "dog paddle." Some dogs are faster swimmers than others.

Why do dogs pant?

Sarah, age 9

When you get hot, you sweat. When dogs get hot, they pant. Panting cools a dog's tongue and mouth. It also cools the blood moving through the dog's body.

Can dogs be friends with cats sometimes?

Matthew, age 9

Do dogs like to play with birds?

Gloria, age 8

Certain dog breeds get along with different kinds of animals better than others. Some dogs are friendly toward cats, birds, and other pets such as ferrets and rabbits. But other dogs will not play with any animal, including other dogs. Some people say it's easier for pets to become friends if they meet when they are very young.

How do they learn to be helpers?

Holland, age 10

Some dog breeds go through special training to help people. Trainers teach dogs to stay focused on their job at all times. Search-and-rescue dogs help people who are lost or in danger. Seeing Eye dogs show their blind owners where to walk. Therapy dogs are trained to be calm and friendly while they keep sick patients company.

When do you give a dog a bath?

Jerry, age 6

Most dogs need a bath about every two to three months. If your dog gets very dirty or rolls in something smelly, it may need a bath more often. Check with your vet for the best kind of shampoo to use.

How do dogs get sick?

Catherine, age 7

A poor diet, lack of exercise, or being near other sick dogs can make a dog sick. Some dogs get sick from eating things they find during a walk. To keep their dogs healthy, owners should take them to the vet for regular check-ups.

How do you know when a dog is full grown?

Bryant, age 6

Most dogs are full grown by 12 months. But they still have a lot to learn!

How do you know when a dog is pregnant?

Sidney, age 7

When a female dog is four to five weeks pregnant, a vet will be able to feel small bumps in its belly. At five weeks, a pregnant dog's belly usually looks bigger. Puppies grow inside their mother for about nine weeks.

How many puppies can a dog have at one time?

Caitlin, age 8

Different breeds have different sized litters. Generally, smaller breeds have smaller litters. The tiny Yorkshire Terrier usually has two to three puppies. A medium-sized Beagle may have a litter of five to seven puppies. Golden retrievers often have six to eight puppies. In 1995, a Saint Bernard had 23 puppies!

What do baby dogs eat?

Emerald, age 9

Puppies drink their mother's milk until they are about four weeks old. After that, they usually eat puppy food.

How many years does a dog live?

Annie, age 8

Smaller breeds usually live longer than larger breeds. Toy poodles and other small dogs live about 14 to 16 years. Medium-sized dogs such as Boxers and Dalmatians live as long as 12 years. Great Pyrenees and other large breeds are expected to live 8 to 10 years.

TO LEARN MORE

More Books to Read

Clutton-Brock, Juliet. *Dog.* New York: DK Pub., Inc., 2004.

Davis, Rebecca Fjelland. *Woof and Wag: Bringing Home a Dog.* Minneapolis: Picture Window Books, 2009.

Simon, Seymour. *Dogs.* New York: HarperCollins Publishers, 2004.

Slade, Suzanne. *From Puppy to Dog: Following the Life Cycle.* Minneapolis: Picture Window Books, 2009.

Internet Sites

FactHound offers a safe, fun way to find Internet sites related to this book. All of the sites have been researched by our staff.

Here's all you do:

Visit *www.facthound.com*

FactHound will fetch the best sites for you!

GLOSSARY

breed—a kind or type within a larger group of plants or animals

coat—the hair or fur on some animals' bodies

litter—a group of animals born at the same time to the same mother

pant—to breathe quickly through the mouth

saliva—a clear liquid produced in the mouth that helps with eating; spit

veterinarian—a doctor who takes care of animals; vet, for short

INDEX

Look for all of the titles in the Kids' Questions series:

Did Dinosaurs Eat People?
And Other Questions Kids Have About Dinosaurs

Do All Bugs Have Wings?
And Other Questions Kids Have About Bugs

How Do Tornadoes Form?
And Other Questions Kids Have About Weather

What Is the Moon Made Of?
And Other Questions Kids Have About Space

What's Inside a Rattlesnake's Rattle?
And Other Questions Kids Have About Snakes

Who Invented Basketball?
And Other Questions Kids Have About Sports

Why Do Dogs Drool?
And Other Questions Kids Have About Dogs

Why Do My Teeth Fall Out?
And Other Questions Kids Have About the Human Body